My name is:

TiLLY

My Brownie

My Six is:

PiXieg

My Brownie friends' names are:

My Brownie Promise

I promise that I will do my best;
To love my God,
To serve the Queen and my country,

To help other people
And
To keep the Brownie Guide Law.

Contents

Have fun with your 2012 Brownie Annual!

Be safe
You should be able to have a go at everything in your Brownie Annual, but sometimes it is a good idea to get some help. When you see this symbol, ask an adult if they can lend a hand.
Be safe

Badges!
Look out for this sign. If you enjoyed the activity on that page, you might like to try the badge too!

Web safe
This symbol means you should follow your Brownie Web Safe Code. To remember it, look it up in your Brownie Badge Book or visit www.girlguiding.org.uk/brownies/websafe.
Web safe

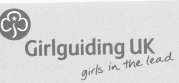
girls in the lead

© The Guide Association 2011
Published by Girlguiding UK
17–19 Buckingham Palace Road
London SW1W 0PT
www.girlguiding.org.uk

Girlguiding UK is an operating name of The Guide Association. Registered charity number 306016. Incorporated by Royal Charter.

Girlguiding UK Trading Service ordering code 6005. ISBN 978 0 85260 251 5

All Brownie and Guide photographs © The Guide Association.
Other photographs courtesy of Shutterstock unless otherwise stated.

Girlguiding UK would like to thank the Brownies and Leaders who took part in the production of this resource. It would also like to thank the London Organising Committee of the Olympic and Paralympic Games for its assistance.

Project Editor: Margaret Swinson
Writers: Steph Burns, Helen Channa, Alison Griffiths, Jenna Harris, Abi Howson, Emma Joyce, Mariano Kalfors, Helen Mortimer, Catherine Murray, Hannah Rainford, Margaret Swinson

Designers: Angie Daniel, Helen Davis, Kim Haddrell, Yuan Zhuang
Cover Design: Kim Haddrell
Production: Wendy Reynolds
Picture Editor: Abi Howson
Project Coordinator: Helen Channa
With thanks to: Ruth Cubitt, Kurt and Jeanette Reitmann, Sandra Bethray
Printed by Scotprint.

Readers are reminded that during the lifespan of this publication there may be changes to Girlguiding UK's policy, or legal requirements, that may affect the accuracy of the information contained within these pages.

Green life is not

Did you know you can grow flowers or vegetables in a pot made from yesterday's newspaper? Follow these step-by-step instructions and get growing!

Plant-Grow-Share has been one of the World Guiding Centenary themes and is featured in the *Together We Can* resource too. Plant-Grow-Share encourages us to raise fresh vegetables for charities that feed people in hospices, homeless shelters and care homes. Visit www.foodshare.co.uk/girlguiding.

☆ you will need:

- ☆ newspaper
- ☆ a wine bottle with a concave bottom
- ☆ scissors
- ☆ soil
- ☆ plant or flower seeds such as marigold or tomato
- ☆ trowel

☆ what to do:

(1) Arrange three sheets of newspaper neatly on top of each other. Lay down the bottle sideways on top of the sheets and cut across the paper, roughly 17cm, so that you get a long strip.

(2) Repeat Step 1 three times so that you have a strip of 9 layers of paper.

(3) Wrap the strips of paper around the bottle, leaving about 3cm of newspaper sticking out below the bottom of the bottle. Holding the end of the newspaper to the bottle, roll the whole length of paper.

clever!

6

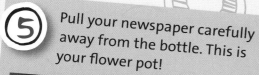
old news!

(4) Now make the bottom of your newspaper pot. Fold in the paper sticking out at the bottom of the bottle.

(5) Pull your newspaper carefully away from the bottle. This is your flower pot!

(6) Fill the pot with soil. Gently press the soil down.

badge

Gardener

link

(7) Poke a hole into the soil about 5cm deep. Plant one seed and cover it with soil. Put the pot on a saucer and give it some water. You can plant the whole pot in the garden when the weather is warm enough.

Super Brownie at the Paralympics

My best Brownie

Think about all the things you did at Brownies this year. Write them down or draw a picture showing what happened.

MY FAVOURITE TRIP WAS...

MY FAVOURITE ACTIVITY WAS...

THE BEST SKILL I LEARNED WAS...

I HAD THE MOST FUN EARNING A BADGE FOR...

haha!

I'LL NEVER FORGET THE TIME WHEN...

To learn more about what Brownies get up to, visit www.girlguiding.org.uk/brownies or call 0800 1 69 59 01 to find out how you can join in the fun.

12

moments

I LAUGHED SO HARD WHEN...

I WAS SO EXCITED THAT I TOLD EVERYONE ABOUT...

I WAS SO SURPRISED...

I NEVER THOUGHT I'D...

THE ACTIVITY I'M MOST PROUD OF IS...

Olympic and

Discover the three Olympic values (excellence, respect, friendship) and four Paralympic values (courage, determination, equality, inspiration) with these challenges!

CELEBRATE 'INSPIRATION'

How many smaller words can you make out of the letters in 'inspiration'?

SEARCH FOR 'EXCELLENCE'

Find the words and phrases in this star word search:

do your best
creative
enterprising
ambitious
focused
organised
wise

```
            D H
          D O W
        E O O E E
        E Y S A
      R H U P C
      W T R O D A
C N M A O N K A I B I D X T H P M P H V
R T U X V Q B K F Y E T G S E H T B H H C
M B C E N D F X S I Q F T G C T E J Y
M X V V X X W T B S F Z W C E T
  B I S Y J U F M H A D S V O A D
    T Y L Q W V A M A S E O N
  I A Y O R G A N I S E D A Z
  G E E N T E R P R I S I N G
O R R E X C C D E S U C O F K O
F V C S G N P     X E T J C W O
D A X K I L U F       X G E H W B B
F N I C W           X C D M Y
P H B E                 X O P Q
```

UNDERSTAND 'FRIENDSHIP'

A Brownie should be all these things. Can you unscramble them?

14

Paralympic values

FIND 'COURAGE'

Have you got what it takes? Find out with this quiz.

1. Games are about... *a*
a) taking part
b) winning
c) eating

2. Winning is more special when I... *A*
a) am honest
b) win by a mile
c) get a prize

3. I face challenges by... *A*
a) being positive
b) being aggressive
c) staying in bed

4. Joining in has helped me become... *A*
a) confident and fearless
b) a Sixer
c) more popular

Mostly As –
You've got the right stuff – keep it up!
Mostly Bs –
You're incredibly competitive! Just remember winning isn't everything.
Mostly Cs –
Oh dear, you're not quite into the spirit of things. Give it another go.

DEFINE 'RESPECT'

Create a poem using a letter to start each line.

R ain or shine, let's do it...
E ven though you are boiling hot you don't
S _____
P _____
E _____
C _____
T _____

SHOW 'DETERMINATION'

Besides hard work and commitment, what will help you to reach your goals? Find two words – inside and outside the star.

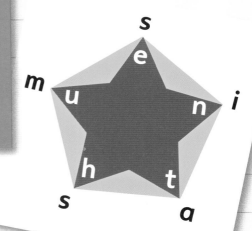

s e n i
m u
h t
s a

PROMOTE 'EQUALITY'

Spot the 8 differences.

15

I was a Brownie, too!

Did you know that lots of famous people were Brownies just like you?

The Saturdays always get us dancing! Most of the girls were Brownies!

What are your favourite Brownie memories?
Frankie I got a certificate for being most like a monkey and when I went away with my Brownies, I got over the tyre wall the fastest!
Rochelle I got a badge for cooking.
Frankie We had a toadstool and you had to skip round it and sing a song.

What do you think about Brownies nowadays?
Una They seem to be having lots of fun.
Mollie It's a good thing to do. There aren't any guys involved – just like us in a girl band! And you can talk about girlie stuff all day.

What talent would earn you a badge?
All Singing!
Frankie A Cooking badge, as I can't cook!
Rochelle I could teach you, I got my Brownie Cook badge!

Charlotte Hawkins has presented television shows for ITN and Sky News, among others.

What did you like about being a Brownie?
Going on Brownie camp was the first time I'd stayed away from home so it was a bit of a daunting experience, but it was also a milestone that was made exciting by being with all my friends.

What badges were you particularly proud of?
I was so excited when I first got my uniform and couldn't wait to start getting some badges for it. I vividly remember preparing for my first badge, the Hostess badge. We learned how to make a proper pot of tea. I didn't drink tea then so it seemed very grown up. I wanted as many badges as possible!

If you could be a Brownie again for a day, what would you do?
I would go back to Brownie camp. It was such a great experience, being with all your friends, playing games and going on outings.

How has guiding influenced your life?
I really believe that the spirit of guiding is a good one to follow. I try to do a good turn every day – holding a door open, helping someone with a pram up some stairs or just taking the time to talk to someone I meet.

TV journalist Kate Silverton has presented everything from BBC News to coverage of the Oscars. She's also gained her Queen's Guide Award.

Tell us about being a Brownie.
I loved my uniform, working to get badges and sewing them on with pride! I loved the camping most, though, as I really enjoyed the outdoors.

What has been your biggest achievement?
I became one of the youngest Queen's Guides, aged 13.

If you could be a Brownie for a day, what would you do?
I would help get more homeless people safe shelter.

Dame Tanni Grey-Thompson has won 11 gold medals in the Paralympic Games and was made a Dame by the Queen in 2005.

What did you like about Brownies?
We worked together on things, and you could be yourself without a lot of adults around.

What advice would you give girls today to help them reach their dreams?
Don't stop trying. Even when something seems too far away, try to achieve it. Brownies teaches you to be organised and determined – these are qualities you need to achieve your goals.

What job might you have chosen?
A lawyer. I like solving problems.

What hidden talent would earn you a badge?
It would have to be Book lover. I have hundreds of books. My favourite book is *The Lion, the Witch and the Wardrobe* by CS Lewis.

How does it feel to have won so many medals?
It's amazing. When you have a good race, it makes every training session on a cold morning worthwhile.

What's your next challenge?
To be a useful member of the House of Lords. I still feel like the new girl in school, still finding my way around and learning the rules. I hope I can make a difference to people's lives.

THEY WERE BROWNIES, TOO!

- Singer Pixie Lott released her first single, *Mama Do*, at 18.
- JK Rowing has sold millions of *Harry Potter* books.
- Ellie Simmonds, MBE, won two gold medals at the Beijing Paralympics at just 13.
- TV presenter Helen Skelton paddled 2,010 miles down the Amazon river in a kayak.

Fairtrade food: Good for

The Fairtrade Foundation has licensed more than 3,000 products in the UK. When you buy Fairtrade food, farmers get a fair and stable price for their crops and workers have decent working conditions. Chocolate, honey, nuts, spices, sugar and fresh and dried fruit come in Fairtrade varieties. Use Fairtrade ingredients for these recipes.

LOOK FOR THIS MARK
fairtrade.org.uk

HONEY-NUT CRUNCH GRANOLA

Five people can share this breakfast.
Note: this recipe contains nuts and is not suitable for people with nut allergies.

ingredients:

- butter for greasing
- 300g oats (any kind)
- 75g almonds, hazelnuts or pecans, chopped
- 130g sunflower seeds, pumpkin seeds, linseeds
- ¼tsp ground cinnamon
- ¼tsp salt
- 60ml water
- 30ml vegetable oil
- 120ml honey
- 3tbsp light brown sugar
- tsp vanilla
- 180g dried fruits
- milk, to serve

① Preheat the oven to 165°C. Grease a deep baking tray with butter.

② Mix the oats, nuts, seeds, cinnamon and salt in a large bowl.

③ Combine the water, oil, honey, sugar and vanilla in a microwave-safe bowl. Heat on high for 1 minute and stir well.

Be safe

④ Pour the honey mixture into the oat mixture. Stir it together.

⑤ Pour the granola on to the tray and smooth it into an even layer. Bake for 15 minutes then stir the mixture. Bake for 15 minutes and stir again. Cool the tray on a wire rack. Sprinkle the dried fruits onto the mix.

you, good for everyone

1 Preheat the oven to 200°C. Grease a baking tray with butter.

2 Cream the sugar and butter with an electric mixer or whisk. Beat in the egg and vanilla until smooth then mix in the flour and ground almonds or currants.

3 Dust a chopping board with flour. Roll out the pastry until it is a ¼cm thick square. Cut it into 8-12 pieces.

4 Put the pastry pieces on to the baking tray. Using a butter knife, spread 1 spoonful of the almond mixture on to each piece. Put the pastries into the fridge for 15 minutes.

5 Ask an adult to cut the apples into ½cm thick slices. Put them in a large bowl and toss with 2 tbsp sugar and cinnamon. Take the pastry from the fridge and lay the apple slices on top of the almond or currant mixture. Fold up the edges of each pastry piece around the apples.

6 Bake the pastries for 20 minutes until the puff pastry is golden.

7 Switch the oven setting to grill or turn on the grill. Grill for 2 minutes.

8 Remove the tray from the oven and cool on a wire rack. Dust the pastries with icing sugar.

APPLE-ALMOND FLYING CARPETS

These pastries will fly off the plate! Makes 8-12.

ingredients:

- ☆ **450g ready-made puff pastry**
- ☆ **50g sugar plus 2 tbsp**
- ☆ **140g butter, softened**
- ☆ **1 egg**
- ☆ **½tsp vanilla**
- ☆ **40g ground almonds or currants (for Brownies with nut allergies)**
- ☆ **1tbsp plain flour**
- ☆ **500g apples**
- ☆ **a pinch of cinnamon**
- ☆ **icing sugar**

Be safe

19

An Adventure for Pearl

Life could be dull when you were the smallest whale in the pod. Pearl was too little to go diving for squid and too young to understand everything the older whales called to each other. So when she heard a low buzzing noise one day, she couldn't wait to check it out.

'Mama! Mama! There's a Noisy Boat!' she cried. 'Can we go and see it?'

Mama listened carefully. She asked her friends what they thought. They didn't hear Noisy Boats very often, and usually Mama wouldn't let Pearl go near them anyway. But maybe...

'All right,' said Mama. 'It's only a small Boat so it may be safe to have a look.'

Pearl swam as fast as she could. Mama was big and strong, and she soon caught up. The buzzing noise grew louder – then it stopped.

'What's happening, Mama? Where did it go?'

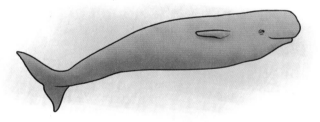

'The Noisy Boat is still there,' explained Mama, 'but it's resting. Look up – can you see it?'

Pearl looked and saw a long shape floating against the ocean's shimmering surface.

'Oooh,' she whispered. 'What are those small things near it, Mama?'

'Those are Humans,' Mama replied. 'They live on Land and on Noisy Boats. Sometimes they swim in the water near us. But we must be careful not to hurt them or frighten them.'

Pearl darted towards the small shapes in the water. The Humans swam to their Boat.

'Oh,' wailed Pearl. 'I wanted to play!'

'I think you scared them!' laughed Mama. 'They are only little. Listen – the Boat is going away.'

'Can we go with it?' asked Pearl.

'No, it's too dangerous for us to go near Land. Come back with me, and I'll tell you why.

'A long time ago, the pod was following currents in the sea. The fish were swimming further north than usual. We went with them into parts of the ocean where we had never been before. We found plenty of squid to eat.

'The sea around us filled with noises: buzzings, chuggings, pings and blips. It sounded as though a thousand Noisy Boats were swimming above us, calling to each other. The noise made our heads ache, but the squid were so delicious that we decided to follow them.

'I made a long dive and caught a tasty squid. When I came back up to the surface for some air, I called to the pod. It was really hard to hear them with all the noise in the water but I thought I heard someone calling back to me. I swam off in that direction.

'As I swam, the noises got even more confusing. I heard snatches of my friends' calls but they were all jumbled up with the Boats' noises and I couldn't tell what anyone was

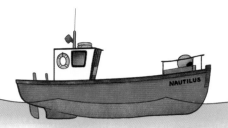

saying. The water was full of echoes bouncing around. I felt very lost and alone.'

'Were you scared, Mama?' asked Pearl, who was feeling a bit scared herself. She tried to imagine being lost, and felt all shivery.

'Yes, I was! I tried to swim back into deeper water but there were Boats everywhere. I started to panic, swimming round in circles, trying to get away. Suddenly a great big Boat came up right beside me. It was churning the water with its sharp metal propeller. A moment later I was slammed into the sand. Rocks scraped against my skin and the hot sun scorched me. I was beached on Land.'

'On Land! What was it like?'

'I was so surprised, I just lay there for a moment, gasping for breath. It felt strangely quiet after the noise of the water. All the sounds were muffled. It felt very wrong, so I took a deep breath and beat my fins as hard as I could. But nothing happened!

'I tried again. Water surged around my sides, but I couldn't move back with it. I thrashed my tail and jerked my body from side to side. Sand and water flew through the air all around me but it didn't do any good.

'I struggled for a long time. At last, with sore fins and tail, I lay still. My back felt parched by the sun. Sharp rocks jabbed my stomach.'

'What did you do, Mama?'

'Suddenly there were Humans around me, moving quickly and making funny babbling sounds. Then I felt cool water flowing over my back! For a moment I thought the sea was

rising around me. But it was the Humans throwing water over me, and it felt wonderful.'

'I felt the Land shifting beneath me and the rocks no longer jabbed into my sides. The Humans were moving them away.

'As the sun sank and the day cooled, more Humans arrived. They began to dig and throw ropes over my back. I let them work – they had been kind to me all day so I had to trust them.

'At last I felt myself sliding backwards into the sea! The Humans pulled me out to deep water and let me go. I was free!

'I heard the pod calling anxiously to me. I called back joyfully and swam to meet them. Then we swam far from that dangerous place.'

Pearl asked, 'So some Humans made you get lost, with their Noisy Boats, then other Humans saved you. Are there two kinds of Humans, good ones and bad ones?'

Mama shook her head. 'Oh no. I think Humans can do harmful things and kind things. We just have to hope that if enough Humans care about the world they will all stop doing things that hurt others. Until then, promise me you will not go near Humans or Boats without me.'

'I promise,' said Pearl. 'Maybe they will start to be kind, and I can play with them.'

'I hope so,' replied Mama. 'That would be good.'

A quiz and a riddle for The

ROUND 1:
See how much you know about The Queen and her reign.

 In what year was Queen Elizabeth II crowned?
a) 1955   b) 1960
c) 1953

 When she celebrates her Diamond Jubilee, how many years will The Queen have been on the throne?
a) 35 years   b) 60 years
c) 50 years

 True or false – The Queen was a Guide when she was younger.

 Which of these crazy gifts has the Queen not received from her supporters and fans?
a) a miniature version of Buckingham Palace
b) a jaguar (the big cat, not the car!)
c) a box of snail shells

ROUND 2:
It's a Diamond Jubilee party and the whole nation is invited! But how will we celebrate?

 What exactly is a Jubilee?
a) an exotic fruit that only grows in certain areas of South America
b) a celebration or time to rejoice
c) an Australian chocolate bar

 How many days in 2012 have officially been set aside to celebrate the Diamond Jubilee (although celebrations could go on all summer)?
a) 2   b) 7   c) 4

 An exhibition of images and paintings of The Queen will go on tour in 2011 to mark the Diamond Jubilee. They will be exhibited in the capital city of each country in the United Kingdom. In which of these cities will it not be on show?
a) Edinburgh   b) Brighton   c) Belfast

 Street parties are a great way of celebrating a Royal Jubilee. See if you can spot the imposter in this list of traditional British party food!
a) cucumber sandwiches
b) popcorn
c) sausage rolls

 The official plan to mark The Queen's Diamond Jubilee is for The Queen to choose a town and...
a) paint a Union flag on all the roofs in the town
b) turn the town into a city
c) give out free chocolate to everyone who goes to Brownies there

Queen's Diamond Jubilee

THE RIDDLE

⭐ what to do:

A DIAMOND NUMBER RIDDLE

This activity is not only a test of your fact-hunting ability, you'll also need some sharp maths skills to crack the code! Write the numbers down as you go along.

1 Take the year in which everyone will celebrate The Diamond Jubilee, and add all the digits together.

2 Add to it the missing number in this fact: The Queen had her coronation in 195___.

3 Add to it the number of children The Queen has.

4 Add to it the date of The Queen's real birthday (it's in April). Write this number down.

5 Find out the year in which Queen Elizabeth II was born. Add the four digits together (to make a two-digit number). Subtract this number from the number you wrote down in Step 4.

6 Add to it the grand old age you have to be to get a telegram of congratulations from the Queen.

7 Finally, add to it the number of queens named Elizabeth in the history of the UK.

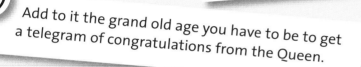

TRICKY NICKNAME

Fill in the gaps to discover the nickname given to The Queen by her family when she was a little girl.

1 The official London residence of The Queen is Buckingham ⌐. (the third letter)

2 We are celebrating The Queen's Diamond ⌐. (the fourth letter)

3 The Queen is part of the ⌐ Family. (the last letter)

4 The last letter of the Queen's favourite type of dog. /

5 The first letter of The Queen's B estate in Scotland.

6 The first letter of The Queen's first name. E

7 The fourth letter in the name of the only other queen to have celebrated a Diamond Jubilee. /

The idea box

This little box will give you lots of ideas for having a great day and sharing good feelings with everyone around you. Take a suggestion from the idea box and do a good turn.

1. Trace or cut out the box on the next page and decorate it any way you like. When the glue is dry, put the box together as directed.

2. Cut a sheet of paper into 2.5cm-wide strips.

3. Write an idea, joke or question on each strip of paper. Below are some suggestions to get you started.

Activities:
Compliment three people today.
Pick up five pieces of litter.
Help make dinner tonight.

Nice thoughts:
Isn't the sky such a lovely colour today?
You've got lots of great friends.
The next Brownie meeting is just around the corner!

Questions:
Can you remember what you dreamed last night?
What was the funniest story you ever heard?
If you could have one wish, what would it be?

Jokes:
How do you catch a squirrel?
Climb up a tree and act like a nut.
Why did the orange stop rolling down the hill?
It ran out of juice.
What do you call a Roman emperor with flu?
Julius Sneezer.

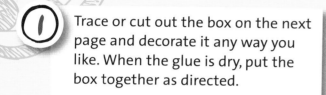

what you need:

- **1 or more sheets of paper**
- **scissors**
- **sticky tape**
- **coloured pens, glitter, stickers to decorate the box**

4. Write until you have used up all the paper or run out of ideas. Tape one end of each strip of paper to the next until you have one long ribbon.

5. Wind the ribbon around itself to make a roll. Keep hold of the end so it doesn't unwind.

6. Put the roll inside the box and feed one end of the ribbon through the slot so that the end pokes out.

7. When you are ready, pull the ribbon until the first idea is out of the box. Tear it off, making sure you leave some the next idea sticking out of the box for the next time.

24

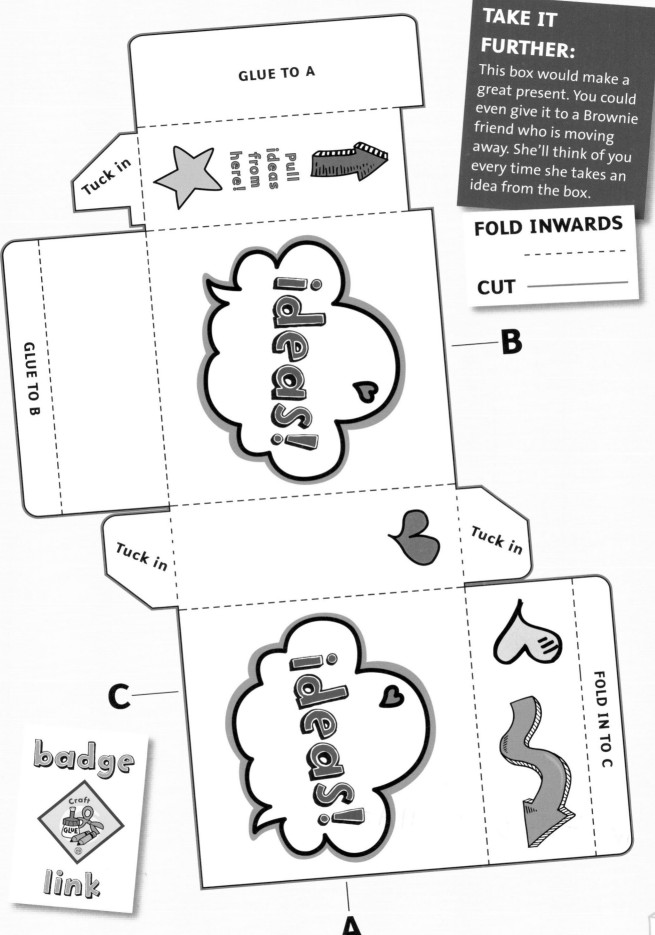

GLUE TO A

Tuck in

Pull ideas from here!

ideas!

GLUE TO B

B

TAKE IT FURTHER:
This box would make a great present. You could even give it to a Brownie friend who is moving away. She'll think of you every time she takes an idea from the box.

FOLD INWARDS

- - - - - - - -

CUT —————

Tuck in

Tuck in

C

ideas!

FOLD IN TO C

badge

Craft
GLUE

link

A

25

Number puzzles

THROWING FISTS

⭐ what to do:

① On the count of three, the players throw their fists out in front of them, extending any number of fingers from 0 to 5. At the same time, one player calls out a number. If the fingers extended add up to that number, the Caller wins.

⭐ what you need:

⭐ at least two players, with one player being the Caller for each turn

② The Caller shouts out a number that might come up. So if there are two players, the number can be between 0 and 10. If three people are playing, the number can be between 0 and 15, and so on. Players must be careful to throw their fists on time so that no one can be accused of changing her fingers after the number is called!

NUMBER CODE JOKE

L	K	Q	H	V	B	C	X	S	R	M	P	U	D	A	W	I	J	F	G	T	E	N	O	Z	Y
1	2	3	4	5	6	7	8	9	10	11	12	13	14	15	16	17	18	19	20	21	22	23	24	25	26

Can you use the code to work out this joke?

16 4 15 21 / 14 17 14 / 24 23 22 /
11 15 21 4 9 / 6 24 24 2 / 9 15 26 /
21 24 / 15 23 24 21 4 22 10?

1 22 15 5 22 / 11 22 / 15 1 24 23 22, /
17 / 4 15 5 22 / 11 26 / 24 16 23 /
12 10 24 6 1 22 11 9!

26

OLYMPIC AND PARALYMPIC MOTTOS

Fill in the remaining numbers in the grid below (B, L, M and T are done for you), then use it to work out the code for each motto.

A	B	C	D	E	F	G	H	I	J	K	L	M	N	O	P	Q	R	S	T	U	V	W	X	Y	Z
	16										26	1							8						

Olympics

20 15 7 8 19 6, 22 23 21 22 19 6, 7 8 6 3 2 21 19 6

Paralympics

7 4 23 6 23 8   23 2   1 3 8 23 3 2

tricky!

badge

link

SWIMMING FISH PUZZLE

☆ you will need:

☆ **8 pencils**
☆ **a button or 5p coin**

☆ what to do:

1 Arrange the pencils in the fish pattern as shown here. Don't forget the coin or button eye!

2 Now rearrange the pencils so that the fish is facing another way – but you can move only two pencils and the eye.

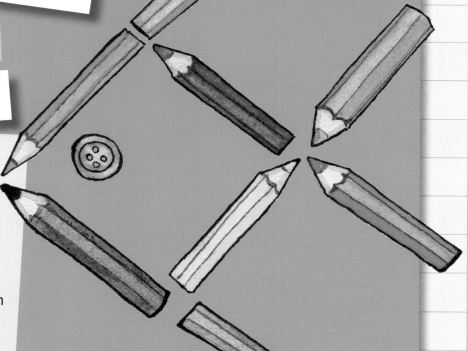

WAGGGS – Friends

The World Association of Girl Guides from 145 countries! Here are six send them on adventures.

Ⓐ
ANTIGUA & BARBUDA:
Brownie (Western Hemisphere)
Fun fact: Every Easter the Girl Guides helps run the Antigua and Barbuda International Kite Festival. The event is part of Caribbean Link Day which celebrates a variety of cultures and includes a kite-flying competition.

Ⓑ
CANADA: *Brownie (Western Hemisphere)*
Fun fact: The Girl Guides of Canada sell 4.4 million boxes of Girl Guides cookies a year. Chocolate-mint cookies are sold in the autumn and chocolate-vanilla sandwich cookies are sold in the spring.

Ⓒ
AUSTRALIA:
Guide (Australia)
Fun fact: Since 1997 all members of Girl Guides Australia are referred to as Guides and all wear the same uniform.

around the world

and Girl Scouts (WAGGGS) has ten million members
Brownies from around the world – cut them out and

SOUTH AFRICA:

Brownie (Africa)
Fun fact: South African Brownies can enjoy a seven-acre Training and Activity Centre (TAC) in Randburg.

PAKISTAN:

Junior Guide (Arab)
Fun fact: The Pakistan Girl Guides Association was founded in 1911 as part of Indian Girl Guiding and became an independent member of WAGGGS in 1948.

REPUBLIC OF IRELAND: *Brigins (Europe)*

Fun fact: There are three levels of Brigins – bronze, silver and gold. Each level has 19 challenges and interest badges.

Cut out the girls and slot them into their matching stands

Explore the

Did you know that there is a special place for Brownies online? The Brownie website is filled with fun, games and stories written by you. Visit www.girlguiding.org.uk/brownies.

BADGES

Find out about the badges Brownies can achieve from the Badges section of the Brownie website. From Agility right through to Writer, there is a badge for everyone.

GAMES

On the Brownie website there are lots of fantastic online games for you to play. You can build a snowman, decorate your dream room or help Detective Brownie solve a mystery – the choice is yours!

BOOK CLUB

Every Brownie is a member of our fantastic book club. Every month there is a review of a book that Brownies will just love! They might be brand-new books or old books that your Mum or older sister read when they were younger. As well as reading the latest review, you can read past reviews of books such as *Candyfloss* by Jacqueline Wilson and *Malory Towers* by Enid Blyton.

ACTIVITIES

Do you like the crafts and games at Brownies? Get some ideas for activities that you can do at home on your own or with your friends.

Brownie website

STORIES

Do you like writing? Here's your chance to get your work published on the World Wide Web. Send us your best story or poem and you might just see it on the Brownie website!

I'll help

ADVICE COLUMN

Are you a good listener? Do you give great advice to your friends when they have a problem? Do you have a problem that you don't know how to solve? If you answered yes to any of these questions, visit the Brownie advice column. Read the problem posted there and then submit your advice to see if you can help out a Brownie friend. If you have a problem, email it in and maybe someone can help you.

THE BROWNIE ONLINE SAFETY CODE

All Brownies should know how to be safe online. Never give out your home address, phone number, the name of your school or any other personal details online.

Always tell a trusted adult if something happens online that upsets or worries you.

Think about using your nickname instead of your real name so that your friends will know it's you but strangers won't.

Don't upload a picture of yourself or your friends online. If you want to use a profile picture, use a cartoon drawing or a picture of your favourite animal.

Don't arrange to meet up with anyone you have met online unless you have permission from your parents or carers and they agree to go with you.

Treat others how you would like to be treated. Just because you can be anonymous online doesn't mean you can be nasty to anyone.

For more help and advice about online safety including chatting, texting and emailing, visit www.thinkuknow.co.uk.

If you or anyone you know is being bullied online, visit www.cybermentors.org.uk.

This icon appears in our Brownie books to remind you to be safe online!

Web safe

See page 36 for our web safety story with Dot Com Brownie.

Recycling is fun

Each year more than 29 million tonnes of rubbish is thrown away in the UK. That's almost five million elephants! But a lot of it can be recycled at home or school. Have fun and recycle at the same time with the activities here!

RING PULL SNAKES

Aluminium fizzy drink cans can be recycled and ready to use in just six weeks. Next time you have a drink, recycle the can after you've finished or reuse it in these creative ways.

you will need:

- ring pulls from cans
- felt or fabric
- red wool
- two eyes for each snake
- glue
- scissors

what to do:

① Cut two long pieces of fabric, no more than 2cm wide.

② Glue the pieces of the fabric together to make a snake.

③ At one end, cut the fabric into a point for the tail.

④ At the other end cut the material into a rounded shape for the snake's head.

⑤ To make the body, thread the ring pulls along the length of the fabric.
- Thread the fabric up through the bigger hole of the first ring pull.
- Then thread the fabric down through the bigger hole of the second ring pull followed by the second hole of the first.
- Repeat with more ring pulls until you reach the tail.

⑥ Glue on eyes and wool for the tongue.

hiss!

CAN JACKET

Think about the label on your favourite fizzy drink. Would you recycle it if the label encouraged you to? Design a label to help promote recycling.

☆ you will need:

- ☆ scissors
- ☆ glue
- ☆ coloured pens
- ☆ paper
- ☆ drinks cans

☆ what to do:

① Cut out a piece of paper 10.5cm x 18cm.

② Think of a slogan such as 'You CAN recycle this!' or 'Start recycling now!'.

③ Write the slogan on the label and decorate it.

④ Put some glue along the back of the label.

⑤ Press the label around the can. It should make a complete circle.

Make a bag

Take your lunch to school, go on a shopping trip or carry your pyjamas to a friend's sleepover with this great bag.

✦ what you need:

- ✦ fabric measuring 64x28cm or larger
- ✦ 102cm of 4cm wide webbing
- ✦ thread to match the webbing colour
- ✦ needle
- ✦ pins
- ✦ scissors

✦ what to do:

① Ask an adult to help you cut out the bag body from the fabric. It will measure 64x28cm.

② Put the colourful side of the fabric face-down on the table. Fold back 1cm on the shorter sides of the fabric and sew this down using a backstitch.

③ Fold the fabric in half across the middle so the hem is at the top and you end up with a square. The fold will be the bottom of the bag. Make sure the bag is still inside-out.

badge

Craft
GLUE

link

34

④ Using a backstitch, sew up the sides of the bag. Cut the webbing in half to make two straps.

⑤ Turn up 4cm of the webbing strap on one end. Pin this end on to the bag's side to keep it in place. Sew the strap end down with a box seam (see photo at left).

⑥ Repeat Step 5 for the other ends of the straps and sew into place. You will have one handle for each side of the bag.

⑦ Turn the bag right-side-out and decorate it any way you like.

Dot Com Brownie

It all started with the girls drawing pictures of monsters during a Brownie meeting. As she reached for a pink pen, Nabila told her best friend Rebecca all about a new website called Feeble Jeebles.

'It's so much fun!' said Nabila. 'You can create a pet called a Jeeble that you can dress up and take for walks to the vet or the park. There are lots of different games and activities you can do. My Jeeble is called Constance. You should create a Jeeble and they could become friends!'

Once Rebecca was home from Brownies, she took the family laptop up to her room and sat down on the floor. She created a Jeeble called Boris. Boris was pink with purple eyes and green hair. He wore a football shirt with yellow shorts and green boots.

A message flashed up on the screen.

'Hi Boris. My name is Constance. Would you like to be friends?'

Rebecca typed back.

to the rescue

'Hi Constance, I would like to be your friend. Thanks, from Boris.'

Boris and Constance were walking in Jeebleland, when another Jeeble approached them and started talking to Boris.

'Hi Boris. My name is Bluebird45. Can we be friends?'

Rebecca hesitated. She didn't know anyone who had a Jeeble called Bluebird45 but she wanted to get as many Jeeble friends as she could. Rebecca typed a message back.

'Hi Bluebird45. I would like to be your friend. Love, Boris.'

Bluebird45 followed Boris and Constance down Jeeble Street and into the Jeeble sweet shop. Another message flashed up on Rebecca's screen.

'Hi Boris. Where do you live and what school do you go to? Love, Bluebird45.'

Rebecca wasn't sure about this. Her Mum had always told her not to tell strangers anything about herself. She looked away from her computer to think about what to do. When she looked back at the computer screen she was amazed to see that the Feeble Jeeble website had disappeared. In its place was a cartoon picture of a girl.

'What's going on?' exclaimed Rebecca.

'I could ask you the very same thing,' said the cartoon girl. 'I think you need some help from Dot Com Brownie!'

The cartoon girl got bigger and bigger until she could no longer fit in the computer. She stepped out of the screen and sat down on the bedroom floor next to Rebecca.

Rebecca stared in amazement. The girl who sat next to her still looked like a cartoon. She had long red hair tied up in a ponytail and big blue eyes. She wore Brownie uniform and pink glittery trainers.

'I'm Dot Com Brownie,' said the girl. 'I'm here to help you make the right decisions when you are online. Have you heard of the Brownie web safe code?'

Rebecca shook her head. She had only just turned seven so hadn't been at Brownies very long.

'The Brownie web safe code will help you make a decision about what to do next. This is what it looks like.' A symbol flashed up on the laptop's screen.

Web safe

Then Rebecca knew the answer to her problem! 'My Mum told me not to give out my personal details to strangers, so I should not answer Bluebird45's question.'

Dot Com Brownie smiled. 'That's right. You don't know who Bluebird45 is, so they could be anyone. You shouldn't give out information about yourself online and if you are not sure or see something that worries you, you should always tell your parents or another responsible adult.'

Rebecca looked sheepish. 'I promise that next time I am unsure about something online I will look at the Brownie web safe code.'

'I think my work here is done,' Dot Com Brownie said. She stood up and dived head-first back into the computer screen. When Rebecca looked at her computer screen again, she saw that the Feeble Jeeble website had returned.

A message flashed up on the screen. This time it was from Constance.

'Hi Boris. Where have you been? Love, Constance.'

Rebecca typed a message back. 'Hi Constance. You won't believe who I've just met! I'll tell you all about it at Brownies next week. From Boris.'

THIS SPECIAL BROWNIE CODE WILL HELP YOU KEEP SAFE WHEN USING THE WORLD WIDE WEB. READ THE RULES BELOW AND USE THEM WHENEVER YOU USE THE WORLD WIDE WEB.

When using the world wide web I promise:

- to agree rules with my parents or carers about the best way for me to use the computer and the world wide web
- not to give out my home address or phone number without permission
- not to give out the name or address of my school without permission
- not to agree to meet anyone who I contact on the web, unless my parents or carers say it is all right and go with me
- not to put my photograph onto a website
- to tell my parents, carers, teacher or Brownie Leader if I find something on the web that worries or upsets me.

With thanks to the Girl Scouts of the USA for ideas contained within this warning for children.

The Big Brownie

Would you like to be a top athlete and listen to the crowd cheer when you win a medal? Or maybe you'd just like to take part in a fun way with other Brownies.

go!

BROWNIE PENTATHLON

The pentathlon is an Olympic contest in which athletes compete in five different events: shooting, fencing, swimming, show jumping and running. The athletes have to be very fit and talented to do well in all these different activities!

Hold your own mini pentathlon. Choose five activities and write them in the table below. Here are some ideas for you to try by yourself or with friends:

⭐ **hula hooping** – how many times can you twirl the hoop without dropping it?

⭐ **doing laps of the garden** – time yourself and your friends with a stopwatch

⭐ **skipping** – how many skips can you do without stopping?

⭐ **throwing and catching a ball for as long as possible** – use your hands, feet or a bat

⭐ **walking on your hands** – how many steps can you take?

⭐ **hopping** – how many hops can you do before you fall over?

⭐ **long jump** – measure how far you can jump with a tape measure or long ruler.

Try each event three times and write down your scores. Can you get better each time? Who has the best score among all the competitors?

My pentathlon scores!

ACTIVITY	1st TIME	2nd TIME	3rd TIME
Skipping			
hula hooping			
Long jump			
Throw and catch			
hopping			

40

Games

BROWNIE GYMNASTICS

Gymnastics has been part of the Olympics since ancient times. Gymnasts use equipment such as rings, bars and vaulting horses, and they also perform an exciting floor routine with lots of acrobatics.

⭐ you try it...

Choose a fun piece of music and make up a gymnastics routine for it. It doesn't matter if you don't know many fancy moves – put in lots of dance steps, jumps and stretches instead! Or try 'rhythmic gymnastics', in which gymnasts use a long ribbon, ball or hoop in their routines.

BROWNIE CYCLING

There are four cycling events in the Olympics: BMX, mountain bike, road and track. Paralympic athletes can take part in road and track cycling on bicycles, tricycles, tandem bikes for two people or handcycles, which are powered by the arms instead of the legs.

⭐ you try it...

Ask an adult to take you out cycling. If there is a local park where you can cycle safely off-road, try doing some timed trials. Do lots of laps of the park and time each lap to see if you can get faster! If you are cycling on roads or cycle tracks, see how far you can go in one ride. Maybe next week you could go a bit further.

badge link

Agility

Cyclist

Always make sure you are wearing a cycle helmet and other protective gear. Check that your bike is in good working order before you ride it. Never go out on your bike without asking first.

Be safe

It's all Greek

The Ancient Greeks did much more than invent the Olympics. They believed in the Muses, nine goddesses who inspired the arts. Many Brownie badges can be linked to the Muses. Ask your Leader if you can work on a badge connected to a Muse.

CALLIOPE
Muse of epic poetry
Symbol:
a wax tablet, an ancient alternative to paper
Badges:
Speaker, Writer, Communicator

CLIO
Muse of history
Symbol:
a scroll, to record information
Badges:
World cultures, Brownie traditions

ERATO
Muse of lyric and love poetry
Symbol:
the cithara, a bit like a harp or guitar
Badges:
Communicator, Speaker, Writer

URANIA
Muse of astronomy
Symbol:
a globe or compass
Badges:
Finding your way,
Science investigator,
Stargazer

THALIA
Muse of comedy
Symbol:
a comic mask with
a smiling mouth
Badges:
Brownie performer,
Entertainer, Circus
performer

TERPSICHORE
Muse of dance
Symbol:
the lyre, an
ancient harp
Badges:
Agility, Sports,
Dancer

EUTERPE
Muse of music
Symbol:
the aulos, an
instrument like a
double flute
Badge:
Musician

MELPOMENE
Muse of tragic theatre
Symbol:
a tragic mask with a
sad or scary face
Badges:
Writer, Entertainer

POLYHYMNIA
Muse of hymns
and mime
Symbol:
a veil, a sign
of nobility
Badges:
Discovering faith,
Circus performer,
Entertainer

Raucous riddles, quirky quips

Do you love a good riddle to puzzle over? Do you enjoy making your friends laugh? Give these a go!

TONGUE-TWISTERS

Fuzzy Wuzzy was a bear,
Fuzzy Wuzzy had no hair,
Fuzzy Wuzzy wasn't very fuzzy,
was he?

Kitty caught the kitten in the kitchen.

Whether the weather be fine
or whether the weather be not.
Whether the weather be cold
or whether the weather be hot.
We'll weather the weather
whether we like it or not.

Fresh fried fish,
fish fresh fried,
fried fish fresh,
fish fried fresh.

The big bug bit the little beetle, but the little beetle bit the big bug back.

Eleven owls
licked eleven
little liquorice
lollipops.

One-one was a race horse.
Two-two was one, too.
One-one won one race.
Two-two won one, too.

JOKES

What do you call a three-legged donkey?
A wonkey!

What's the strongest vegetable in the world?
A muscle sprout!

Knock, knock!
Who's there?
Emma.
Emma who?
Emma bit cold out here
– will you let me in?

What is black and white, black and white, black and white?
A zebra caught in a revolving door!

What do dogs eat at the cinema?
Pup-corn!

44

MORE JOKES

What do you call a sleeping dinosaur? A dino-snore!

gross!

Why was the nose sad? Because it never got picked!

How do you cut the sea in half? With a sea-saw!

Why do chickens sit on their eggs? They don't have chairs to sit on!

Where do books sleep? Under their covers!

Why can't you tell a cow a secret? Because it will go in one ear and out the udder!

What's brown, hairy and wears sunglasses? A coconut on holiday!

RIDDLES

How many letters in the alphabet? Eleven (t h e a l p h a b e t).

A cowboy went on a trip on Friday, stayed three days, and came back on Friday. How is that possible? His horse is named Friday!

What kind of ship never sinks? Friendship.

S.S. FRIENDSHIP

I have streets but no pavement, I have cities but no buildings, I have forests but no trees, I have rivers yet no water. What am I? A map!

What kind of coat does a house wear? A coat of paint.

Create your own Big

Why not organise your own Big Brownie Games (see pages 40-41) to celebrate and take part in the 2012 competitions? You can even create some home-made awards!

CROWNING THE WINNER

Did you know the Olympics started in Ancient Greece? Winners were crowned with wreaths of olive leaves instead of being given medals. Make this crown and you'll have a great prize to give the winners of the Big Brownie Games.

(see pages 40-41)

⭐ what you need:

- ⭐ green paper
- ⭐ glue
- ⭐ scissors
- ⭐ rulers
- ⭐ pens
- ⭐ sticky tape

⭐ what to do:

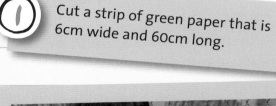

1 Cut a strip of green paper that is 6cm wide and 60cm long.

2 Get a Leader or a friend to help you measure it around your head to work out how long it needs to be. Mark the spot and cut the paper to the right length.

3 Cut out lots of leaf shapes from the green paper. The original wreath looked like this.

Cool!

4 Making sure to leave space at either end, stick the leaves on to the band with glue. It looks really great if you use different shades of green paper.

5 Using sticky tape, tape the two ends of the band together. This crown should fit just about any Brownie.

46

Brownie Games awards

These days we give medals to the winners of the Games. Try these for yourself.

⭐ what you need:

- ⭐ air-hardening clay
- ⭐ rolling pin
- ⭐ cookie cutters
- ⭐ drinking straw
- ⭐ gold and silver paint
- ⭐ paintbrushes
- ⭐ grease-proof paper
- ⭐ ribbon

⭐ what to do:

1 Using a rolling pin, roll out a small piece of clay until it is as thick as a pound coin.

2 Use a cookie cutter to cut out a circular piece.

3 With the drinking straw, punch a hole at the top of the circle (where the ribbon will go through).

5 Carefully move your medal on to a small piece of greaseproof paper. Leave your medal to dry.

4 Using a butter knife or other blunt edge, mark 1 or 2 on the medal before it dries.

6 When the clay is dry, paint it gold or silver.

7 Thread some ribbon through and tie the two ends together.

badge

Craft
GLUE

link

47

A Brownie's

Katy and Jasmine love being Brownies but they're about to turn ten – so what's their next adventure going to be?

The 2nd Anywhere Brownies are ready to start their meeting.

We've got news!

Our birthdays are on the same day. In June, we're both going to be ten.

I'd really like to go on to Guides as soon as I'm ten. Can I?

Yes! You can choose to move to Guides when you are ten and when you feel ready.

That's great! We'll help you celebrate and plan a party.

What if I'm not ready?

Later on at Brownies

Ellie, what's it like being a Guide? Do they have games and trips like Brownies?

In lots of ways Guides is just like Brownies, but there's a big difference – we're a bit older and we get to plan more and make more of our own decisions.

transition to Guides

Next week, before Brownies

Home time!

Later on at Brownies

50

Snowy Owl, I think I have an idea to help Katy feel better about going to Guides.

Two minutes later.

Great idea! I'll speak to Ann at 1st Anywhere Guides and invite them to Jasmine's and Katy's birthday party as a surprise.

Jasmine's and Katy's last week at Brownies.

Happy Birthday!

Jasmine and Katy, we have some surprise guests for you.

Happy Birthday!

Let's play a party game. Katy, would you like to be my partner?

Yes please! I know – Jasmine, let's show them our game.

If being a Guide is anything like the fun I've had today, it's going to be the best!

Nature detective

THE COUNTRY MOUSE AND THE CITY MOUSE

As our towns and cities grow, space for wild animals gets smaller. Animals that once lived in rural places are now finding homes in parks and gardens.

You can become a nature detective no matter where you are. Start in your own garden – a birdbath or birdfeeder will be very active. If you live in a city, look for other green places.

Here are some animals that have become expert urban wildlife.

what you need for these activities:

- ☆ notebook
- ☆ pen or pencil
- ☆ magnifying glass
- ☆ small jar or bag
- ☆ field guide

Birds:
pigeon, peregrine falcon, seagull, duck, goose, swan, heron
Small mammals:
rat, mouse, rabbit, grey squirrel, hedgehog, bat
Larger mammals:
fox
Reptiles and amphibians:
grass snake, frog, toad
Insects:
stag beetle, cricket, spider, butterfly, dragonfly

Find these animals in the country or by the sea.

Birds:
puffin, eagle, owl
Small mammals:
red squirrel, dormouse
Larger mammals:
seal, otter, badger, red deer
Reptiles and amphibians:
lizard, adder, newt
Fish:
basking shark, pike, salmon

MAKE YOURSELF INVISIBLE

Sshhh

Even animals that live in a noisy environment will be wary of humans. You will be able to spend more time watching them if you make as little noise as possible, keep still, wear clothes that are not brightly coloured and hide behind something while you are watching. Practise sneaking up on your friends and you'll soon get the hang of it!

SIMPLE ATTRACTION

There are many ways to lure wildlife to you. Put out bread or seeds on a windowsill for the birds. Moths are attracted to light, so sit next to an upturned torch in the garden one evening. You can make a birdhouse, bat box or bee box fairly easily.

badge link

Seasons

Wildlife explorer

A BIRD'S-EYE VIEW

Falcons have fantastic eyesight. Foxes have a powerful sense of smell. Bats use echolocation to detect food. Use a magnifying glass to examine a patch of grass, a tree trunk or a leaf. How would different animals use their senses when encountering it?

THINGS TO REMEMBER

Be safe

Never touch a wild animal, no matter how cute it is. If frightened, it may try to bite you. Spend as much time as you can observing it and enjoying its beauty instead. Wash your hands once you've finished a nature adventure.

GO ON A JOURNEY

Follow an ant or bee as it goes about its business. Can you discover its nest or hive? Some insects travel great distances to find food. You can plant a window box with some bee-friendly flowers.

A SOUND DIARY

An animal's call or a bird's song is its 'signature'. Keep a diary of all the sounds you can hear. Many animals like foxes are nocturnal and you are more likely to see or hear them after dark or early morning.

A COLOURFUL SKETCHBOOK

Make drawings of the animals you discover, either while you are watching them or afterwards. A guidebook will help you identify them.

A NATURE TABLE

Doing the activities on these pages, you may find some amazing things: a feather, a leaf, a wild flower, a piece of bark, a seedpod. Set up a special place for your collection.

TAKE IT FURTHER:

Many animals die after eating rubbish. Ask your Leader to organise a Brownie clean-up day. Take a few plastic bags and pick up litter at a park. You'll be amazed at the difference!

Be safe

Express yourself!

Do you want to tell people what you think? Here's how to make your voice heard...

YOU MIGHT WANT A SAY ABOUT...

- ✰ what activities are offered at Brownies
- ✰ changes at school like shorter playtime or new rules about packed lunch
- ✰ local issues – perhaps a play-park is closing
- ✰ changes to a food or a product you like or don't like
- ✰ a TV programme, film or product you think is not suitable.

badge
link

WHAT HANNAH DID

At Hannah's Brownies there was always a lot of sporty stuff going on. Hannah liked this but she and some of her friends decided they would also like to do their Cook badge. At the next Pow-wow they asked to discuss what activities they did at meetings and then they voted for doing cooking. By the end of term all the Brownies had their Cook badge!

WHAT GENEVIEVE DID

Genevieve wanted to walk to school but there were no pavements for half of the journey and it wasn't safe. Genevieve's dad helped her write to the local council. She asked them to put some pavements in. The council said that they would look at the problem. In the end, instead of new pavements, a 'walking bus' was set up so that Genevieve and her friends could walk to school in a big, safe group.

WHAT ROSE AND FLEUR DID

Rose and Fleur hated doing maths! At the next school council meeting they told the headmaster that maths should not be taught as it was too hard. The headmaster told them how useful maths is in life, but he discussed different ways to teach the subject with the teachers. Before too long Rose and Fleur were enjoying doing much better at maths!

WHAT ASHA DID

Asha and her brother heard that their local forest was going to be sold and houses built on the land. They loved playing in the forest and watching the wildlife so they joined their mum at a meeting about the forest and signed a petition. Eventually the forest was saved!

PREPARATION, PREPARATION, PREPARATION!

- ⭐ Work out what you want to say first.
- ⭐ Check your facts – make sure what you say is true and not just how you imagine it.
- ⭐ Think about how your outcome affect others.
- ⭐ Get support. If lots of people feel the same way, you are more likely to make a change.
- ⭐ Think about consequences. What will happen if you do or don't get your way?
- ⭐ Decide what you are prepared to do to help make something happen. If your mum agrees to you keeping a guinea pig, are you prepared to put your pocket money towards caring for it?
- ⭐ You have a right to speak up about things that concern you but you also have a responsibility to listen to others' opinions and answers to your concerns. There may be good reasons that mean you cannot do what you'd like.

Sometimes you won't be able to change things. This happens to everyone. Try to make small changes so that the situation is not so bad.

WAYS AND MEANS

- ⭐ Have your say at your next Brownie Pow-wow.
- ⭐ Talk to your class's council rep.
- ⭐ Write to a newspaper.
- ⭐ Write to your local MP.
- ⭐ Email the company that makes the product you are concerned about. Check out the product's packaging for a contact address.

Detective Brownie

I was closing up for the day – Scruff was so desperate to go to the park the pot plant was getting nervous – when there was a knocking at the door. It sounded like Morse code.

-... . .- - - ... . .--. .- .-. -.- .. -. - . -.
-- .. -. .. - . ...

I grabbed Scruff's lead and he just about fainted with excitement. As I locked the door I swear I heard the pot plant sigh with relief.

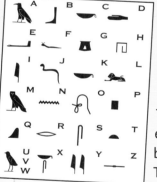

Morse code

A	•−	N	−•
B	−•••	O	−−−
C	−•−•	P	•−−•
D	−••	Q	−−•−
E	•	R	•−•
F	••−•	S	•••
G	−−•	T	−
H	••••	U	••−
I	••	V	•••−
J	•−−−	W	•−−
K	−•−	X	−••−
L	•−••	Y	−•−−
M	−−	Z	−−••

The park was emptier than school on Sunday. Scruff started barking at a tree. I walked over to see why the hairy mutt was fussing. I saw some strange marks on the tree: hieroglyphics! Good thing archaeology is a hobby of mine...

The park was deserted, like everyone had been abducted by aliens. (More on that later.) The sky turned stormy.

Hail pelted down in huge icy stones. When it stopped I looked at the ground and my jaw hit the floor. There was a message was spelled out!

RETURN THE KEY OR PERISH

Crikey, was I glad I paid attention in geometry class! Then a cricket perched on the end of my nose and started to sing. He seemed to say something in the middle of all the buzzing:

ZZYZZOZZUZZMZZUZZSZZTZZFZZIZZNZZDZZ
ZZTZZHZZEZZKZZEZZYZZ
ZZGZZOZZTZZOZZTZZHZZEZZZZZZOZZOZZ

By golly, was I glad I had cleaned my ears this morning! We caught the bus and went straight to our destination.

It was after visiting hours but the zoo was in chaos. The animals had been let loose and the keepers were nowhere in sight. Then I noticed a series of numbers scrawled on the ground.

666539 46873

By George, I was glad I had brought my mobile! As we made our way through all the animals I could hear my gut telling me something. Well, two things actually. One was that I hadn't eaten since lunch, and two was that some monkey business was going on.

The monkey pen was occupied by King Louie, self-appointed Lord of the Jungle, Master of Mayhem, Sultan Orang-utan of Bhutan.

'I should have known you'd be involved, King Louie. Did you set everyone loose? Where are the zookeepers? You know a thing or two about this missing key, don't you?'

'I don't know anything, Detective B. I'm just in here minding my own business.'

'Spill the beans, Louie, or I'll send Scruff in there.'

Louie sighed. 'I tell you what, if you solve my riddle, I might just throw you a bone or two.'

'What is in seasons, seconds, centuries and minutes but not in decades, years or days?'

and the missing key

Ha! You'd have to catch me pretty early in the morning to trip me up on that one. I gave Louie the answer and watched him sulk. 'A deal's a deal, you big ape. Now spill.'

'I'm a primate of my word so here's your clue.'

'If you take a "kettle" and replace the first letter with the answer to the riddle then you'll know what to look under. You dig? And when you get there, just remember, the number is "key".'

I figured out the answer in a second. But who'd willingly look under THAT? Ouch! I remembered passing by one on the way in to the zoo. We went back to the first spot.

'Dig, Scruff,' I told him. That dog was keen. Ten minutes later Scruff's claws hit something: a small box. It had a three-digit combination lock. Hmm... What was Louie's clue again?

'The number is "key".'

I checked my mobile keypad then dialled the combination. The lock sprung open.

I looked inside. A key. Maybe the kind that opens all sorts of doors? Even cage doors?

Scruff and I had work to do! We herded the animals back in their pens and locked them up with the special key. I double-locked Louie's door. We found out where the zookeepers were. Seems they had accidentally locked themselves in the lion's den - smart move! We set them free and they scurried home without even a thank you. Adults – I tell you!

Suddenly an alien saucer came to a

halt above us. A little door opened and a hand reached out.

I grabbed the key and threw it up in the air. The tiny green arm caught it. Then the alien saucer was gone.

'Nice work, I knew I could count on you.'

I turned around to see who was talking to me. 'Is that you, Wally Woodpecker? So you're the one who's been leaving all those clues.'

'Sorry about all the skulduggery I didn't want Louie to know I'd been snitching.'

'So what's been going on?'

'We always get the odd ETs coming round to visit the zoo. One dropped that key by Louie's pen and he let everybody out.'

'Well, if that scoundrel gets up to any more mischief, you let me know.'

Wally waved. 'So long, Detective. And thanks again.'

Turn to page 77 for the answers.

Brain-teasers!

NUMBER TRIANGLE

Rearrange the numbers in each circle so that the total on each side equals 9.

clever!

1 + 9 = 10
+ 6 = 16

BIRTHDAY BONANZA

Add together all the digits in your date of birth. So, if you were born on 7 October 2003 (7/10/2003), add together 7 + 1 + 0 + 2 + 0 + 0 + 3. Your answer is 13. Can you find someone else with the same sum as you?

58

SUDOKU

Although Sudoku puzzles are made up of numbers, there is no maths involved. You just need to work out where the numbers go – that's what makes it fun. Once you get the hang of it, you may find yourself wanting to do more and more of these brain-teasers!

the rules:

Each line of boxes going across the grid must have numbers 1-6.

Each line of boxes going down the grid must have numbers 1-6.

Each of the six boxes shown with darker lines must have numbers 1-6 in them.

There is only one right way to finish each puzzle, and if you think carefully you will be able to work out the answer.

2	1			4	3
		6	2		
		3	4		
3	4			5	6

d	s	d	i	c	z	a	b	a	l	l	a
i	d	j	k	a	a	x	a	q	o	a	t
v	i	k	o	d	b	v	a	l	u	m	d
d	s	j	p	v	a	t	i	d	o	o	i
h	t	r	i	b	w	i	h	a	u	l	v
e	r	a	a	h	a	u	s	k	a	a	e
w	a	z	f	b	c	n	k	h	e	r	r
e	c	j	o	m	u	b	l	u	k	o	s
t	t	o	v	o	d	i	s	t	a	a	i
d	i	v	e	r	t	i	m	e	n	t	o
s	e	s	h	o	v	y	c	l	o	d	n
o	d	i	t	r	e	v	i	d	d	g	y

BROWNIE FUN WORD SEARCH

Brownies is all about having fun! Can you find the word for 'fun' in these different languages?

zabava (Croatian)
sjov (Danish)
lol (Dutch)
hauskaa (Finnish)
divertimento (Italian)
moro (Norwegian)
zabawa (Polish)
divertido (Portuguese)
distractie (Romanian)
diversion (Spanish)
kul (Swedish)

The milky way

Growing bones need lots of calcium. You can find it in dairy products like milk, yoghurt, cheese and ice cream. Ask an adult to help with these recipes.

1 Preheat the oven to 200°C.

2 Combine the yoghurt, flour, sugar, oil, milk and salt in a large bowl and mix thoroughly.

3 Beat the eggs and milk in a small bowl and add them to the large bowl. Stir thoroughly and mix in the cherries or peel.

FLUFFY YOGHURT MINI CAKES

There are so many flavours of yoghurt such as strawberry, lemon, vanilla, peach and apricot. Why not try them all! This recipe makes about 30 mini cakes.

☆ ingredients:

- ☆ **175ml yoghurt (any flavour)**
- ☆ **370g self-raising flour**
- ☆ **150g sugar**
- ☆ **100ml vegetable oil**
- ☆ **¼tsp salt**
- ☆ **3 eggs**
- ☆ **a splash of milk**
- ☆ **150g glacé cherries or candied peel**
- ☆ **fairy cake cases**

4 Fill the fairy cake cases three-quarters full with cake mixture. Bake for 15 minutes and test. They are done when a knife inserted into the centre comes out clean.

CRUSTLESS MILK TART (MELKTERT)

If you like rice pudding you'll love this creamy dessert from South Africa. After one bite you'll be saying, 'Dat smaakt lekker!' – That tastes good!

⭐ ingredients:

- ⭐ 2tbsp melted butter, plus more for greasing
- ⭐ 2 eggs
- ⭐ 175g sugar
- ⭐ 500ml milk
- ⭐ 115g plain flour
- ⭐ 1tsp baking powder
- ⭐ ½tsp ground cinnamon
- ⭐ a pinch of salt

1. Preheat the oven to 175°C. Grease a large pie dish with butter.

2. Crack the eggs carefully and beat with an electric mixer or whisk. Add the melted butter, sugar and half the milk.

3. Sift the flour, baking powder, cinnamon and salt into the egg mixture with a sieve. Mix everything together gently but thoroughly with a wooden spoon. Add the rest of the milk.

4. Pour the mixture into the pie dish and bake for 45 minutes. The tart is done when a knife inserted into the middle comes out clean. It can be eaten hot or cold.

badge

Cook

link

If you liked these recipes, why not try *The Brownie Cookbook*? It's available for £4.30 at www.girlguiding shop.co.uk (code 6840)

It's great to be me!

PERFECTLY UNIQUE

What makes you special? How are other people special in different ways? If you think about it, you'll see our differences make us unique, and that makes us pretty special.

☆ you will need:

- ☆ **old magazines and newspapers**
- ☆ **scissors**
- ☆ **glue**

☆ what to do:

① Collect magazine and newspaper pictures of girls' or women's faces that you think are pretty.

② Cut out the bits of each face that you think are prettiest. A girl in one picture might have really glossy hair; one may have sparkling eyes. Lay all these parts together to create a new face (or several).

Does the final picture still look 'pretty'? Do you think anyone could have ALL those features? No one is perfect but everyone has features that make them unique and beautiful!

FREE TO DREAM...

Have you ever thought about what your future might hold? There are so many wonderful surprises in store – but you can start thinking about them now!

☆ you will need:

- ☆ **collage materials**
- ☆ **pens**
- ☆ **paper**

I NEVER KNEW THAT!

Sometimes we have trouble seeing ourselves but other people can be good at pointing out the best in us. Here's an activity to help us look again at ourselves and our friends. Ask your Leader to help with this game.

what to do:

1. At Brownies, everyone writes their name on a slip of paper and puts it in a hat. (Make sure everyone's name goes in.)

2. Your Leader muddles up all the slips and everyone takes one and a sheet of paper. Look at the name on your slip and write down three good things about that Brownie. Write the person's name at the top of the paper. But don't tell anyone!

3. The Leader collects all the sheets of paper and hands them out to the right people so everyone can see what is written about them. There will probably be some things on that had never realised before!

what to do:

1. Think about what your life will be like in the future. Everyone has a different dream. What will you do for a job? Will you have a house? Will you have pets? Think about how things will have changed. Will we all have space cars? Can you make up any funny inventions?

2. Draw a picture or make a collage of yourself in the future.

63

Squishy cushion

Find some great fabric and get sewing!

⭐ notes:

The seam allowance is 1.5cm.

⭐ you will need:

- ⭐ a piece of fabric measuring 88x58cm
- ⭐ scissors
- ⭐ thread
- ⭐ pins
- ⭐ stuffing material

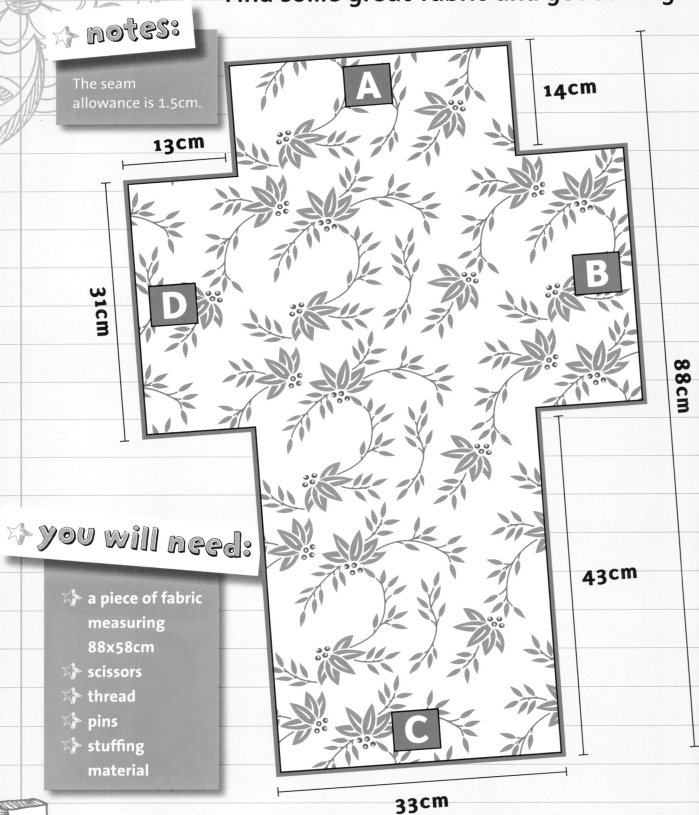

14cm

13cm

31cm

88cm

43cm

33cm

A

B

C

D

⭐ what to do:

1 Ask an adult to help you measure and mark the cutting lines on the fabric as shown. Cut out the fabric.

2 Turn the fabric face-down. Pin the nearer side of panel A to panel B and sew them together using a back stitch.

3 Pin the nearer side of panel A to panel D and sew them together with a back stitch.

4 Pin the other side of panel B to panel C and sew them together.

5 Pin the other side of panel D to panel C and sew them together. You will now have something that looks like a box with an open lid

6 Sew up two sides of the box. Stuff the cushion with stuffing material until it is firm. Sew up the last side with a whip stitch.

Competition

Tell us about the fun you're having at Brownies and win one of these prize packs!

SPORTY FUN PACK:

- ✩ Wenlock, the London 2012 Olympic Mascot stuffed toy
- ✩ Mandeville, the London 2012 Paralympic mascot stuffed toy
- ✩ *The Official Countdown to the London 2012 Games* book
- ✩ London 2012 headband and hair clip set
- ✩ London 2012 pictogram football

Prizes kindly donated by The London Organising Committee of the Olympic and Paralympic Games

COOKING FUN PACK:

- ✩ *The Brownie Cookbook*
- ✩ 6 stacking beakers
- ✩ melamine tray
- ✩ apron
- ✩ *The Brownie Book of Summer Fun*
- ✩ *Brownie Stripes* series, books 5-7

COMPETITION RULES:

- ✩ Make a list of 10 new things you've done at Brownies and the 3 best things in your 2012 Brownie Annual.
- ✩ Tell us your name, age, address, Brownie unit and which pack you would prefer.

SEND YOUR ENTRY TO:

Brownie Annual 2012 Competition, Girlguiding UK, 17–19 Buckingham Palace Road, London SW1W 0PT. The closing date for the competition is **28 February 2012**.

- ✩ Visit www.girlguidingukshop.co.uk to buy these Brownie items.
- ✩ Visit www.london2012.com to learn about the 2012 Olympic and Paralympic Games.

Brownie shopping

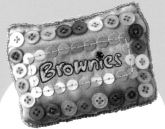

BROWNIE BUTTON PURSE
7128 £3

MUG
8182 £2.55

I LOVE BROWNIES BEAR
2014 Available from
September 2011
£5.11

MINI WIND UP TORCH
7139 £2.04

HAIRBRUSH
8315 Available from
September 2011
£5.60

BROWNIE PHOTO FRAME
7120 £3

'ME TO YOU' MOCK LAYER T-SHIRT
8118 – 8120
£12

I LOVE BROWNIES TEDDY CLIP
2022 Available from
September 2011
£3.06

'ME TO YOU' ORDER CODES BY SIZE/STYLE

CHILD AGE	6-7	8-9	10-11	12-13
MOCK LAYER T-SHIRT	8118	8119	8120	-

A world full

COFFEE FILTER RAINBOW

Have you ever thought about how colours mix to make other colours? Yellow and blue make green. **Chromatography** is a way of saying 'separation' or 'un-mixing' and it means 'to write colour'. With this experiment you'll discover that black ink contains a whole rainbow of colours!

what you need:

- ✦ a non-permanent black felt-tip marker pen
- ✦ a white paper coffee filter
- ✦ a drinking glass
- ✦ scissors

1 Cut around the border of a coffee filter so that it becomes two halves.

2 Draw a horizontal line across the middle of one filter with the pen.

cool!

5 Wait 20 minutes for the filter paper to soak up the water. As it does, the water will separate the ink into its different colours.

3 Pour an inch or two of water into the glass so that the bottom of the filter paper can rest in it.

4 Put the filter into the glass so that the bottom of the paper touches the water and the ink is dry above it.

6 Remove the filter from the glass. Let it dry on a piece of kitchen roll. How many colours can you see?

# of colour

badge

link

what you need:

- a square of muslin
- 1 beetroot, chopped, or a handful of blackberries
- ½tsp white vinegar
- a pinch of salt
- 1 tea bag or 1 fruit tea bag
- lemon juice or 100ml milk
- a drinking glass
- white paper
- a thin paintbrush
- a candle

PURPLE INK

Wrap the beetroot or blackberries in the muslin and squeeze over a glass. You may want to wear washing up gloves as the juice will stain your skin. Stir in the vinegar and salt, which will help to preserve the colour. Now use the paintbrush to write with the ink.

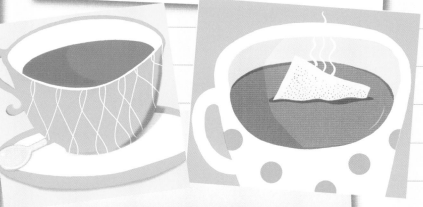

BROWN OR PINK INK

Place a tea or fruit tea bag in a mug half-filled with boiled water. Steep for 3 minutes then use the tea as ink.

INVISIBLE INK

Write your secret message in milk or lemon juice. It will disappear! To read it, hold the paper carefully over a candle.

Be safe

69

Word games

THE MINISTER'S CAT

This is a great game to play when it is raining or you are on a long journey.

There are two ways to play, and you can play with as many people as you like.

GAME 2

1 Player 1 begins the game, choosing an adjective that begins with A to describe the cat. For example: 'The Minister's cat is an **A**stounding cat.'

2 Player 2 must choose an adjective that begins with B. 'The Minister's cat is a **B**eautiful cat.'

3 Each player gets a turn to choose an adjective and continue through the alphabet.

4 The game continues until a player can't think of an adjective. This player is out and the game continues until only one person remains and wins.

☆ how to play:

GAME 1

meow

1 Player 1 begins the game, choosing an adjective that begins with A to describe the cat. For example: 'The Minister's cat is an **A**mazing cat.'

2 Player 2 must also choose an adjective that begins with A. 'The Minister's cat is an **A**gile cat.'

3 Each player gets a turn to choose an adjective beginning with A.

4 Once everyone has had a go, Player 1 chooses an adjective that begins with B.

5 The game continues until a player can't think of an adjective or chooses one that has already been said. This player is out and the game continues until only one person remains and wins the game.

Take it FURTHER

TAKE IT FURTHER

You can speed up the game to see if everyone can keep up. Or why not try a new sentence? 'My mother's tea set was **A**ntique.' 'My mother's tea set was **B**roken.'

READING BACKWARDS

These sentences read both ways:

'Was it a car or a cat I saw?'
'Step on no pets.'
'A nut for a jar of tuna.'
'Did Hannah see bees? Hannah did.'
'Ma has a ham.'
'No lemons, no melon.'

Here are some words that mean one thing forwards and another thing backwards:

stressed/desserts
gateman/nametag
deliver/reviled
straw/warts
star/rats
lived/devil
diaper/repaid
smart/trams
spit/tips
stop/pots
was/saw

Is your name *Hannah, Anna, Ava* or *Eve*? Do you live in *Glenelg* (Scotland), *Serres* (Greece) or *Apapa* (Nigeria)? Have you ever taken a trip in a *kayak* or a *racecar*? Now spell these words backwards. A **palindrome** is a word or sentence that can be read backwards and forwards and still say the same thing.

Write a story with some secret palindromes. Here's an example to tickle your funnybone. 'In *Liam's mail* there was a coupon for *lion oil* at the *llama mall*. But when I got there, there was *no trace, not one carton!* So instead I bought *UFO tofu* and an *evil olive*.'

STEP ON NO PETS

THE ALPHABET IN A BAG

This game is a great way to improve your memory. It starts, 'I packed my bag and in it I put...'

☆ how to play:

1) The first player begins by choosing an object that begins with **A** to take on a trip. The sillier the item is, the better. For example: 'I packed my bag and in it I put an **A**ntelope.'

2) The next player must continue the list and add an item of her own that begins with **B**. 'I packed my bag and in it I put an **A**ntelope and a **B**anana.'

3) The list continues until one person forgets an item or can't think of a new one. This player is out. The game goes on until one player remains and wins.

Fun at the Training and

Archery
Bungee trampoline
Canoeing
Dragon boating
Explore London from ICANDO
Fencing
Grass sledging
High ropes course
Inflatables

Jumping
Karaoke
Low ropes course
Mountain biking
Nightline
Orienteering
Pond dipping
Quick walk
Rafting

Swimming
Trampoline
Urban camping
Visit a new place
Waddow's Warren
eXtremely fun
Yelling at the top of your voice
Zip wire

Did you know that there are eight guiding Training and Activity Centres (TACs) around the UK? Brownies can visit with their units or families to take part in some amazing games and activities. You can even have a birthday party or stay overnight!

ICANDO

Who would have thought that you could go camping in the middle of London! There's also a giant tent, indoor karaoke and a puppet theatre.

BLACKLAND FARM

This TAC in East Grinstead caters for every need – all the activities except rock climbing are suitable for everyone, including people with disabilities. Try them for yourself!

LORNE

Lorne is a great place for exciting outdoor activities with your Brownie friends. It is near Belfast, Northern Ireland, and is close to a mountain, a lake and the sea.

HAUTBOIS

Fancy going pond-dipping or canoeing? How about pioneering or braving the aerial runway? Have a special day out at this TAC near the Norfolk coast.

Activity Centres

WADDOW

Waddow is huge! If you want some adventure in Clitheroe, try the brand-new zip wire, or if you like exploring up high, go rock climbing or jump on the trampolines.

NETHERURD

This TAC is in the Scottish border hills. You can go for night walks, try environmental activities in the conservation hut and have fun in the giant inflatable Earthball.

BRONEIRION

Wales offers beautiful countryside as well as endless mountains. Broneirion is the perfect place for pony-trekking, walking holidays and Brownie camp.

To learn more about what Brownies get up to, visit www.girlguiding.org.uk/brownies or call 0800 1 69 59 01 to find out how you can join in the fun.

FOXLEASE

Foxlease has 65 acres of New Forest land perfect for camping, archery, abseiling, climbing, canoeing, kayaking and crate challenge.

Lorne

Netherurd

Waddow

Hautbois

Broneirion

ICANDO

Foxlease

Blackland Farm

Put your best

For centuries different cultures have used appearances to guess about personality types. Have some fun and find out what makes your face special. You should always love the way you look!

FACES

Round
Those with round faces are smiley and cheerful. People love your friendly nature.

Square
Square-faced girls never give up. You also aren't afraid to stand up for what you think is right.

Oval
People with oval faces are calm and able to see both sides of a situation.

Long
If you have a long face you're charming and polite.

PUCKER UP!

Full lips
If you have large lips you are a confident, chatty person who may find it difficult to keep quiet for long!

Small lips
Small lips mean you are good at keeping secrets - but you can also be a bit shy.

Upturned mouth
In your world every day is sunny and you beam with optimism.

Downturned mouth
At first people may think you're a bit serious, but if you smile they will soon see your fun side.

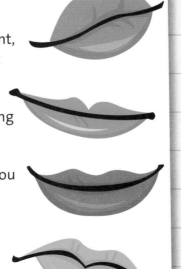

ALL ABOUT HAIR

Redheads have strong personalities that others are drawn to. They have been painted by many famous artists who admired their locks for their rare colour.
Blondes are sweet, likeable and intelligent.
Brunettes are reliable, enthusiastic and outgoing.
Straight hair? Friends are often jealous of your smooth mane which reflects your inner calm.
If you have **curly or wavy hair** you are determined and good at reaching goals.

face forward!

GRIN AND SAY CHEESE!

If you have **gappy teeth** you are a lucky girl.

Crooked teeth can indicate stubbornness.

Straight teeth mean that you're hardworking.

CHINS, EARS AND NOSES

Lucky you if you have a large nose – it shows cleverness and success.

Don't worry if your nose is small as it means you are considerate, quiet and determined.

A large chin means ambition and determination.

Small-chinned people are good at following instructions and paying attention.

Large ears can indicate a strong and successful person. If you have **small ears** you are kind-hearted and quiet.

EYE SPY!

Green eyes are said to mean passion but also jealousy. In mythology, many magical characters have green eyes.

Brown-eyed girls are trustworthy, calm and good at sports.

Blue eyes represent kindness but you can be a bit of a daydreamer.

Hazel-eyed people are considerate, clever and like challenges.

FOREHEADS

A **small forehead** represents a kind and selfless person.

If you have a **high forehead** you're good at problem solving.

Answers

P22-23: Diamond Jubilee

The Diamond Jubilee quiz –

Round One
1. c
2. b
3. true
4. a

Round Two
1. b
2. c
3. b
4. b
5. b

A diamond riddle –
1. 2+0+1+2 = 5
2. 3
3. 2
4. 21
5. 1+9+2+6 = 18
6. 100
7. 2
Final answer: 115.

Tricky nickname –
1. pa**L**ace
2. Jub**I**lee
3. Roya**L**
4. Corg**I**
5. **B**almoral
6. **E**lizabeth
7. Vic**T**oria

lilibet
(Lilly
b4)

P26-27: Maths puzzles

Number code joke

Answer - What did one maths book say to another?
Leave me alone, I have my own problems!

Olympic and Paralympic mottos

Olympic - Faster, Higher, Stronger
Paralympic – Spirit in Motion

P56-57: Detective Brownie

Knock - BE AT THE PARK IN TEN MINUTES
Hieroglyphics - YOU ARE BEING WATCHED. FIND COVER
Hailstones - RETURN THE KEY OR PERISH
Cricket - YOU MUST FIND THE KEY. GO TO THE ZOO
Phone numbers - MONKEY HOUSE
Riddle - The letter N
Kettle - Kettle minus K plus N equals NETTTLE
The number is 'key' - 539

P78-79: The Big Brownie Games

P58-59: Maths puzzles
Number triangle

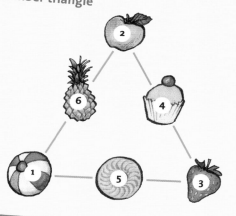

P14-15: Olympic and Paralympic Values 'Spot the difference'

Sudoku

2	1	5	6	4	3
6	3	4	5	1	2
4	5	6	2	3	1
1	2	3	4	6	5
5	6	1	3	2	4
3	4	2	1	5	6

Brownie fun word search

d	s	d	i	c	z	a	b	a	l	l	a
i	d	j	k	a	a	x	a	q	o	a	t
v	i	k	o	d	b	v	a	l	u	m	d
d	s	j	p	v	a	t	i	d	o	o	i
h	t	r	i	b	w	i	h	a	u	l	v
e	r	a	a	h	a	u	s	k	a	a	e
w	a	z	f	b	c	n	k	h	e	r	r
e	c	j	o	m	u	b	l	u	k	o	s
t	t	o	v	o	d	i	s	t	a	a	i
d	i	v	e	r	t	i	m	e	n	t	o
s	e	s	h	o	v	y	c	l	o	d	n
o	d	i	t	r	e	v	i	d	d	g	y

The Big Brownie Games

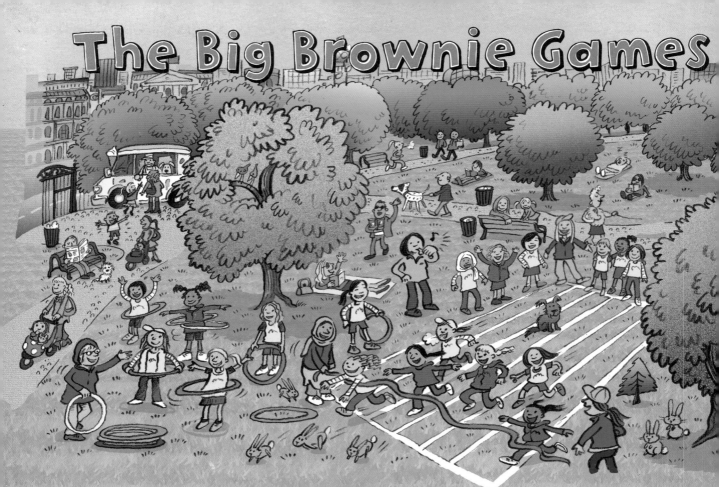